The Lost Orb

BY DAN SHELLEY

ILLUSTRATED BY RACHEL BEDEL

BLOCK ISLAND FERRY

TICKETS

Mom, thanks for always
encouraging my crazy
adventures and supporting me.
This is for you.

LOVE YOU.

No part of this publication may be reproduced, stored in a retrieval system, or transmitted in any form or by any means, electronic, mechanical, photocopying, recording (including but not limited to story-time videos), or otherwise, without written permission from the publisher. For information regarding permission, contact: Dan Shelley: DanShelley@shelldaart.com

Illustrations and layout design by Rachel Bedel | Published by: Dan Shelley | Printed in the USA | ISBN: 9798362625153

While on the ferry headed to Block Island, Ashley was dreaming about her summer vacation! The beach is her favorite place. She loves to feel the warm sun on her face!

While eating ice cream,
Ashley overheard kids
talking about finding shiny
orbs. Ashley had never
heard of an orb but loved
finding treasures.
She was excited!

The next morning Ashley was walking the beach with her mom and asked, "What's an orb?"

Mom said, "An orb is a gorgeous glass ball that shimmers in the Block Island sun. With excitement Ashley said, "That sounds like fun!"

Every year, an artist named Eben
creates and hides these glass orbs
all over the island. One time he
even hid one under a chair!

Families love coming to Block Island and looking for them! They are hidden all over the island! Maybe under a tree? One thing we know is they are always by the sea.

Ashley looked with excitement high and low for the glass orbs from the Lighthouse to the Painted Rock. She was upset that she searched nonstop for all seven days of their vacation and couldn't find any, even after hours and hours. She also checked between the flowers!

The vacation was quickly coming to an end. Ashley was sad because she looked everywhere! She even looked in the library just around the bend.

Ashley decided to keep looking and

went around

and around

and around

the statue in the center of town!

She was sure she would find an orb behind a big chocolate bar at the candy store. Just like the Painted Rock, she came up short but wanted to look just a bit more.

As Ashley was getting
ready to board the
Ferry, she turned
around to give one
last look at her
favorite summer spot.
It was then she saw
something shiny,
right there in the lot!

Ashley tugged on her mommy's shirt
and said, "Look, mommy!" They
dropped their suitcases and ran
up the stairs. Chasing that bright
shiny thing next to all the chairs.

Under a chair at the top of the stairs, there
it was lying in the grass! Ashley finally
found that magical piece of glass!

Ashley showed everyone! What a wonderful way to end a magical vacation with her family at her favorite place, Block Island! Now it's time to look forward to the next summer filled with fun! For now, it's time to say good night to the sun.

ABOUT THE ARTIST

Eben Horton first tried his hand at glassblowing when he was 9 years old. That experience inspired him to ask for an after school job at the same glass studio when he was 15. When he first started his after school job, they handed him a broom and he cleaned the studio while he watched the team of glassblowers make their work. Slowly, Eben learned from them how to make simple things and eventually became a confident glassblower.

One day when he was 19, a days worth of glass paperweights were rejected due to minor flaws inside them. Eben decided to take them all and hide them along the beaches of Rhode Island. 30 years has passed since this first hiding of glass and Eben still finds great joy in providing a fun activity for people to do on block island.

Eben's glass studio - The Glass Station is in Wakefield, RI which is a 12 minute drive from the Block Island ferry dock in Point Judith. The website for The Glass Station is:
www.theglassstationstudio.com.

ABOUT THE AUTHOR

Growing up in southeastern CT, Dan Shelley has always been a life long lover of the beach. On a recent trip to Block Island with his family, this story came to him while searching for orbs. He immediately went back to the beach house and wrote this story!

The beach is a special place for Dan and his family. Some of his fondest memories are from days under the sun with his toes in the sand.

This is Dan's first book and he is already excited for future projects!

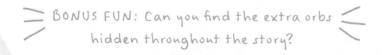

BONUS FUN: Can you find the extra orbs hidden throughout the story?

Made in United States
North Haven, CT
13 December 2022